AF575382

GENDER EQUALITY

by Marie des Neiges Léonard
and Sara Cucini

LIGHTBOX
openlightbox.com

Lightbox is an all-inclusive digital solution for the teaching and learning of curriculum topics in an original, groundbreaking way. Lightbox is based on National Curriculum Standards.

STANDARD FEATURES OF LIGHTBOX

AUDIO High-quality narration using text-to-speech system

VIDEOS Embedded high-definition video clips

ACTIVITIES Printable PDFs that can be emailed and graded

WEBLINKS Curated links to external, child-safe resources

SLIDESHOWS Pictorial overviews of key concepts

TRANSPARENCIES Step-by-step layering of maps, diagrams, charts, and timelines

INTERACTIVE MAPS Interactive maps and aerial satellite imagery

QUIZZES Ten multiple choice questions that are automatically graded and emailed for teacher assessment

KEY WORDS Matching key concepts to their definitions

MORE Extra information and details on the subject

FIRST HAND Letters, diaries, and other primary sources

DOCS Speeches, newspaper articles, and other historical documents

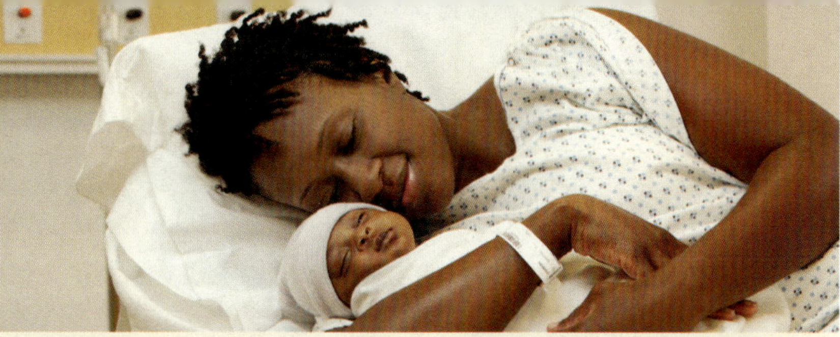

Table of Contents

CHAPTER 1

The significance of gender varies around the world. On Sumatra, Indonesia, the Minangkabau people, whose crafts include weaving, are organized in community houses controlled by a head woman, her sisters, and their daughters.

Understanding Gender

Gender refers to a social classification of individuals into categories that each society constructs in connection with the differences between males and females. Many societies divide those differences into two genders. They are feminine and masculine.

Gender also refers to the physical, behavioral, and personality traits that a particular society considers to be appropriately masculine or feminine. For example, some societies might define masculinity as being more aggressive and competitive, and femininity as more emotional and nurturing. Other societies might have different expectations and **norms**. These characteristics are not biologically determined. They are constructed by societies and cultures. These norms create shared ways of thinking about what males and females in a society or culture can and cannot do.

Gender socialization is the process of learning the social expectations and attitudes associated with one's gender. It contributes to gender inequality by reinforcing ideas about social norms and practices that place males and females in different positions in terms of their access to power, wealth, and other resources. By linking power and gender, these social norms directly impact how individuals think of themselves and their potential to act in relation to power.

2015
Year that Target retail stores eliminated "Boys" and "Girls" signs in their children's departments.

4 Million
Total population in Indonesia of the Minangkabau people, the world's largest group that traces descent through the mother.

Less Than One-half
Portion of British toy shops that separate their toys by gender.

ACTIVITIES

Video

Gender Norms: Always Limiting, Sometimes Deadly | Lisa Cravens-Brown | TEDxOhioStateUniversity

Assess the importance of gender norms and their effects on the lives of men and women.

1. Compare and contrast how gender norms affect men and women. Why might gender norms have an impact on the professional and social lives of women? What effects do gender norms have on men and boys? Why are these effects different?
2. Do you agree that "socially constructed gender norms are always limiting, often harmful, and sometimes deadly"? Why or why not? Defend your point of view.

Weblink

What is gender socialization and why does it matter?

Evaluate the consequences of gender socialization by reading this article.

1. Why does gender socialization "contribute to inequalities in education, employment, income, empowerment"? Do these inequalities affect both male and female individuals? Explain your answers.
2. What are the "agents of socialization"? Why are they "influenced by factors such as the socio-economic conditions of a country, gendered and political structures, social and cultural norms, the global media, and [...] local communities and networks"? Support your answer with examples.

While most world cultures were founded on and are governed by ideas about male superiority, **matriarchies** do exist in specific areas. These areas include parts of Tibet, Indonesia, Ghana, Kenya, and Costa Rica. Some matriarchal societies pass property and power through female family members.

Gender in the World

Gender norms are different throughout the world, and they have varied throughout history. In Western European fashion of the 18th century, masculine attire included a wig, a hat with feathers, breeches and stockings, a ruffled long-sleeved white shirt, and square-toed shoes with ribbons and bows. In recent times, these styles are no longer considered traditionally masculine.

Links between gender and color in fashion have also changed over time, particularly in societies influenced by Western European culture. As colored fabric became cheaper and more widely available, fashion leaders began to assign clothing colors to different genders. By 1918, pink was a typical color for boys' fashion, but that had changed by the 1940s, when clothing designers started to promote blue as a color for boys and pink for girls.

The popularity of separate colors for boys and girls has declined somewhat in recent years. In 2017, the British retail chain John Lewis added a **gender-neutral** clothing collection for young children. The same year, the Swedish clothing-retail company called H&M announced the introduction of a **unisex** line of denim products. In the 21st century, gender often does not determine the way people dress.

Today, discussions about gender norms in the world go far beyond fashion. The World Economic Forum, an international nonprofit organization based in Switzerland, runs an annual conference for public-private cooperation that addresses various global issues. One issue the group studies is how the **gender gap** affects societies by limiting female participation in the economy, education, health, and politics.

Socialization

Socialization is the process of learning and internalizing the cultural norms, values, and beliefs that exist in one's society. In this way, individuals become functioning members of their society. In some societies, **gender roles** are a part of socialization.

The process of gender socialization takes place principally through families, schools, peers, and the media. Families are the primary source of socialization. After birth, gender socialization takes place through the choice of clothes, room decorations, toys, and even bedtime stories. Also very important is the role played by others in the family as well as those people outside the family who interact with the child. All family members teach the child about gender norms through expectations and everyday interactions.

Gender socialization pervades all aspects of family life. It could be seen in everyday chores given to either boys or girls. Boys might be asked to mow the lawn, for example, while girls are asked to wash the dishes. Socialization of children can also be seen in what activities they might be encouraged to do and in what color or style of clothes they are allowed to wear. Research shows that caregivers rely on these social norms to show what society considers to be appropriate behavior. The end result is that all through childhood, children are internalizing the gender expectations of others around them and those of the larger society.

At school, girls and boys frequently play in same-sex groups and often have gender-stereotyped games. Also, research shows that teachers, both male and female, interact differently with students according to their gender. In preschool and kindergarten classrooms, for instance, boys may be prompted to choose sandboxes and building blocks for play, while girls may be encouraged to use kitchen centers.

Research shows that, in the elementary grades, girls tend to outperform boys academically. However, among middle school students, studies show a decrease in girls' interest and achievement in math and science, compared to boys. Most researchers attribute this decline to gender socialization, and a number of schools have taken steps, in recent years, to counter the trend. Middle-school educators have had success with various approaches to closing the gender gap in math and science. Some schools try to provide female role models and mentors from science, technology, engineering, and math (STEM) careers. Teachers may also organize hands-on science-related or math-related activities after school for groups of their female students.

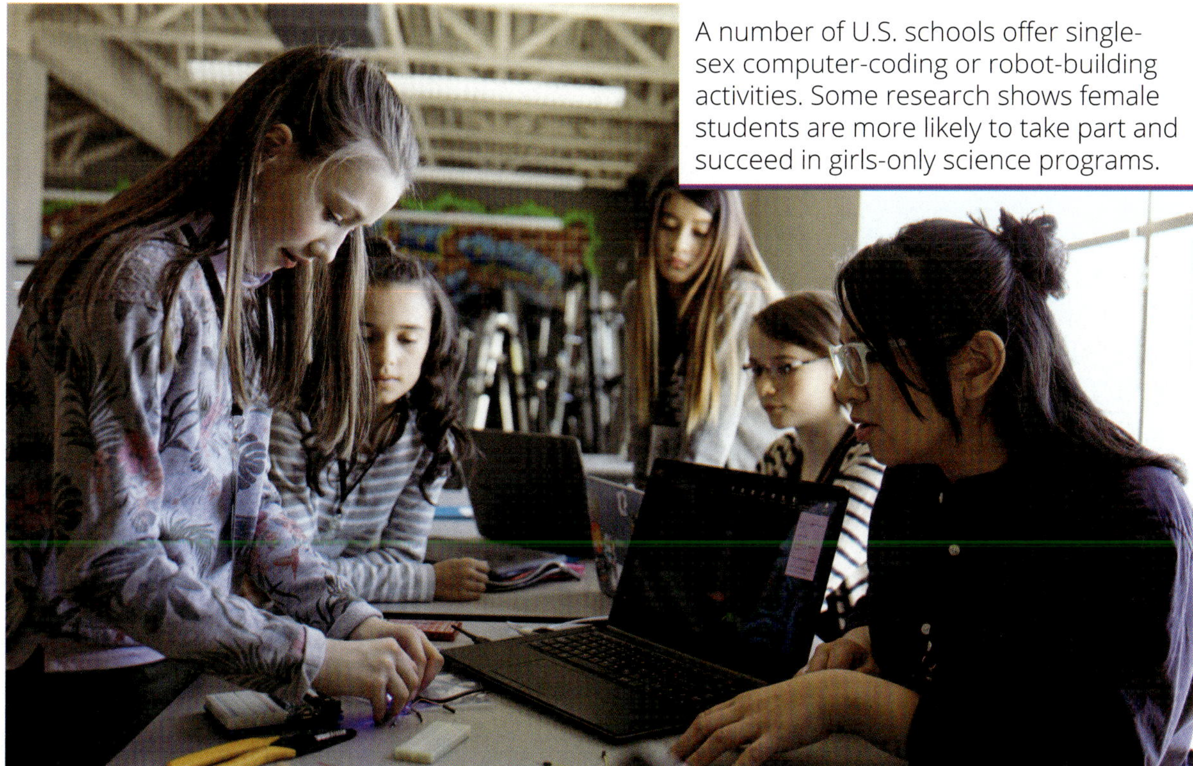

A number of U.S. schools offer single-sex computer-coding or robot-building activities. Some research shows female students are more likely to take part and succeed in girls-only science programs.

ACTIVITIES

Weblink

Men's Fashion in the 18th Century.

Analyze the characteristics of men's fashion in 18th-century Western Europe, and how it differs from contemporary fashion.

1. What were the characteristics of 18th-century fashion in Western Europe? In your opinion, why was men's fashion characterized by these features? Did all members of society adopt this style? What was the purpose of this fashion style? Explain your answer.
2. How do contemporary and 18th-century men's fashion differ? How did gender norms influence the evolution of fashion? Support your answer with examples.

RUBRIC

Analyzing a Journal Article

Students will assess a journal article and write an analysis. An exemplary analysis will meet the following criteria.

- Identifies the topic of the article
- Identifies the main points and opinions presented in the article
- Identifies the writer of the article
- Presents information about the writer and infers how his or her life may have shaped this opinion
- Assesses the writer's reliability
- Analyzes how the writer makes his or her argument
- Uses evidence from the article to show how the writer supports his or her argument
- Analyzes the writer's use of literary devices to enhance the article
- Differentiates between the facts and opinions presented in the article
- Identifies when and where the article was published, and determines its intended audience
- Identifies and understands the goals of the article
- Assesses the effectiveness of the format in presenting the writer's argument
- Connects the article to the societal and historical context in which it was written
- Infers what is not said about this topic in the article
- Identifies what information is unintentionally implied in the article
- Uses correct spelling, grammar, and punctuation

Peer groups have become, in recent times, an increasingly important agent of socialization in most Western societies. By the age of three, children are more likely to play with same-sex playmates. Research shows that same-sex peer groups can reinforce traditional gendered behavior. For example, same-sex children's activities are more likely to be gender-typed than activities engaged

Gender and Language

Language is an element of culture and the primary means through which we communicate with one another. We use language to construct meaning in society, so language also shapes our perception, or the way we see things. Studying language can show us the way norms are constructed. Masculine and feminine differences are reflected through language. For instance, some words for positions of power and authority, as well as for positions requiring strength and stamina, emphasize the male gender but are presented as if they were gender-neutral. These terms include "congressman," "chairman," "policeman," "fireman," and "fisherman." The implication here is that one gender is more suited than another to perform the job.

In the English language, there are expressions that seem to assume that the default category for human experience is male. The human race is often referred to as "mankind," and people say "all men are created equal." Other similar terms include "manmade," "manslaughter," or "manpower," as if the male experience represented all people. These terms came to be accepted as gender-neutral nouns. Sometimes, gender markers are attached to jobs. Some people might refer to a "woman pilot," "woman astronaut," "male nurse," or "male teacher." The application of gender markers shows gender bias, or preference or prejudice toward one gender. Often, when people say "male nurse" or "woman police officer," they signal that they are seeing an apparent inconsistency or disconnect between the occupational role and the gender of the individual doing the job.

Especially in the 21st century, language and word usage have changed somewhat. It has become more common to refer to the head of an organization as simply the "chair." Gender-neutral terms for occupations, such as "police officer," "firefighter," and "fisher," are more widely used. However, use of older terms persists, and this usage continues to influence the gender socialization of males and females.

in by boys and girls playing together. In addition, violating gender norms can sometimes be challenging for young people.

All forms of media, including movies, comic books, popular music, and social media platforms such as Instagram, Twitter, and Facebook, teach children what is accepted and valued in society. Explicit and implicit messages about gender help establish standards of behavior and role models. These messages simultaneously communicate expectations about gender roles.

Gender Roles

Roles in society can be defined as a set of behaviors expected from someone who holds a particular status. For example, a person who is a professor is expected to be a responsible teacher and researcher. Firefighters and police officers are expected to be physically strong, and people count on nurses to be caring and knowledgeable in emergency situations.

The roles a society expects of its members include gender roles. Each society's gender roles are transmitted and learned, and they are relative to particular cultures that hold certain expectations for their own women and men. For example, some societies might expect men to show their masculinity by being aggressive and competitive and expect women to show their femininity by being nurturing. The cross-cultural evidence shows a wide variation of behaviors for the sexes. In the popular Bollywood movies produced in India, audiences expect the male hero to cry, and the best actors are those capable of showing emotion.

More than 90 percent of American teenagers access the internet daily. The internet and social media play an influential part in establishing gender roles.

Dig Deeper

Consider the way you have been socialized by your family, your school, or society. Collect information about what toys you played with as a child, what extracurricular activities you were encouraged to do, and what household chores you did. Share your experiences with another classmate, and write an essay comparing and contrasting the information.

ACTIVITIES

Document

Can Gender-Fair Language Reduce Gender Stereotyping and Discrimination?

Analyze the journal article about gender-fair language and its benefits.

1. What are the main strategies adopted to make different languages "gender-fair"? Do you think these strategies are equally effective? How do they differ? How are they similar? What other strategies could be adopted? Formulate some hypotheses.
2. Do you agree with the idea that gendered language promotes stereotyping and discrimination? Why or why not? Defend your position.

RUBRIC

Create a Map

Students will create a map of a relevant topic. An exemplary map will meet the following criteria.

- Has a clearly distinguishable title (e.g., larger letters, underlines) that tells the purpose/content of the map
- Labels and locates all items correctly
- Includes a legend that is easy to find and contains a complete set of symbols, including a compass rose
- Scales all features correctly and clearly indicates the scale
- Uses correct spelling and capitalization
- Uses color appropriate for features (e.g., blue for water; black for labels)
- Includes properly documented sources

Gender Equality around the World

In 2006, the World Economic Forum (WEF) designed the Global Gender Gap Index to measure gender equality in the nations of the world. Each year, countries are evaluated and ranked for the degree of equality for women in four areas. These are educational attainment, political empowerment, health and survival, and economic participation and opportunity. The WEF's 2017–2018 Global Gender Gap Report covered 144 countries. The United States ranked 49th.

LEGEND

Global Rankings of Gender Equality

- 1st to 36th
- 37th to 72nd
- 73rd to 108th
- 109th to 144th
- Not included

SCALE

N

0 — 1,200 Miles
1,200 Kilometers

Mexico, ranked 81st in the WEF Gender Gap Index, has tripled the number of women serving in its army and air force. In 2018, the nation's armed services included almost 19,000 women, about 7 percent of Mexico's total troop strength. The federal government, in Mexico City, has set a goal to further increase the number of women serving in the military.

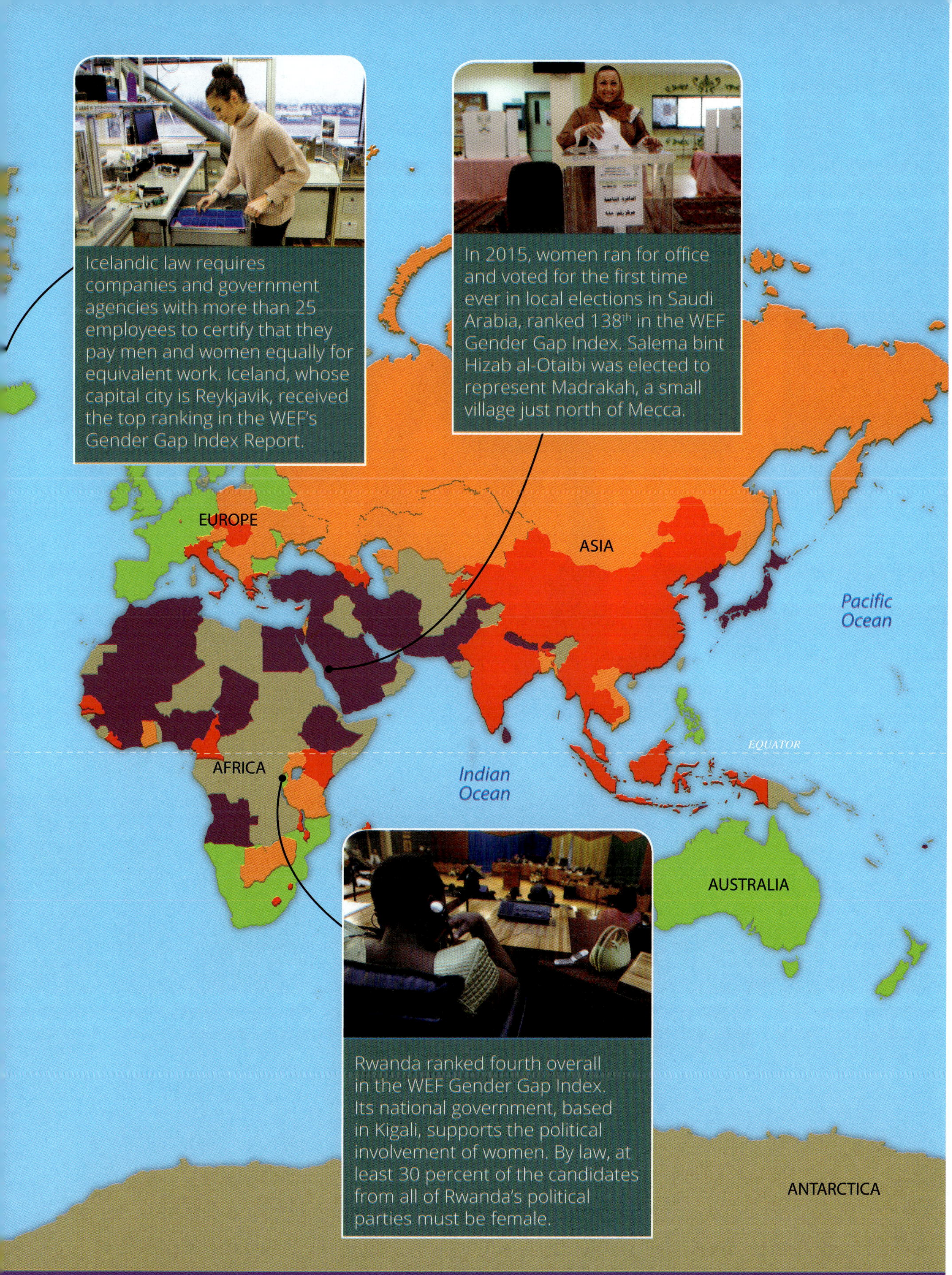

Icelandic law requires companies and government agencies with more than 25 employees to certify that they pay men and women equally for equivalent work. Iceland, whose capital city is Reykjavik, received the top ranking in the WEF's Gender Gap Index Report.

In 2015, women ran for office and voted for the first time ever in local elections in Saudi Arabia, ranked 138th in the WEF Gender Gap Index. Salema bint Hizab al-Otaibi was elected to represent Madrakah, a small village just north of Mecca.

Rwanda ranked fourth overall in the WEF Gender Gap Index. Its national government, based in Kigali, supports the political involvement of women. By law, at least 30 percent of the candidates from all of Rwanda's political parties must be female.

ACTIVITIES

Google Maps

Gender Equality around the World

Compare and contrast gender equality in some of the countries ranked by the World Economic Forum.

1. Does the location of each country influence its Global Gender Gap Index? Would its Global Gender Gap Index change if it were located on another continent? Why or why not?
2. What do the countries characterized by a low ranking or a high ranking in the Global Gender Gap Index have in common? Are these similarities significant or not? Why?
3. What changes or improvements have countries with a low ranking in the Global Gender Gap Index implemented? What other solutions could be adopted to improve gender equality in these countries? Formulate some hypotheses.
4. In your opinion, why is gender equality important? What consequences could gender inequality have on the lives of people? Support your answer.

RUBRIC

Analyzing an Interview

Students will listen to and assess an interview related to a historical or cultural event, and write an analysis of what they have learned. An exemplary interview analysis will meet the following criteria.

- Identifies where and when the interview took place
- Identifies the subject of the interview
- Describes how the interview is presented
- Gives examples of the information provided by the interview
- Summarizes the information and opinions presented by the subject of the interview
- States whether the information is a firsthand or secondhand account
- Assesses how easy or difficult the interview is to understand
- Organizes the analysis in a logical, effective manner
- Makes inferences about the experiences of the interview subject
- Compares the interview to other sources about the same event
- Cites all sources used in the analysis
- Uses correct spelling, grammar, and punctuation

CHAPTER 2

In democratic countries, gender equality includes ensuring equal voting rights for men and women. In the United States, more women than men have voted in every presidential election since 1964.

Gender Rights Movements

Gender differentiation refers to social processes that construct and exaggerate biological differences to distinguish activities, interests, or attitudes as either male or female. These patterns are part of a larger system of gender inequality. A gender hierarchy places women and men in different positions in terms of power, wealth, and other resources. Throughout history, women in many cultures have fought, and continue to fight, to assert their power and establish gender equality.

Gender equality issues include equal pay for men and women doing the same type of work, equal access to all categories of jobs and promotion to all levels of responsibility, equal educational opportunities, and equal access to and quality of health care. The concept of gender equality is a core element of democratic societies. Nevertheless, gender inequality permeates all cultures and manifests itself through laws, policies, institutions, and everyday practices.

Women define their own interests and goals differently in different parts of the world. Therefore, various women's movements have advocated for the rights of women. In European and North American democracies, the women's movement fighting for gender equality developed in three waves.

More Than 500,000
Membership of the American activist organization the National Organization for Women (NOW).

Less Than One-third
Number of U.S. states in which women could vote in all elections before American women gained the right to vote nationwide.

1981
Year Sandra Day O'Connor became the first female justice on the U.S. Supreme Court, 191 years after the Court heard its first cases.

ACTIVITIES

First Hand

'Out of Order' At The Court: O'Connor On Being The First Female Justice

Read this interview, and analyze the importance of Sandra Day O'Connor's nomination as Supreme Court Justice.

1. O'Connor stated that she felt "a special responsibility" as the first female Supreme Court justice. In your opinion, was this feeling justified? Do you think she would have felt the same feeling, had she been named nowadays? Why or why not?
2. How did being a woman influence O'Connor's career? Would she face the same challenges nowadays? Do you think O'Connor would have retired to take care of her spouse, had she been a man? Why or why not? Explain your answers.

Weblink

This Day in History: National Organization for Women was Founded

Evaluate the history of the National Organization for Women.

1. When was NOW founded? Why was it founded in this specific historical period? What were the main fields of action of NOW? Why was NOW active in these fields during its first years?
2. Have the interests and work of NOW changed over time? Why or why not? Support your answer with examples.

RUBRIC

Create a Chart

Students will create a chart illustrating a concept. An exemplary chart will meet the following criteria.

- Includes an appropriate title and headings
- Has neat and legible chart lines, boxes, and text
- Contains accurate content
- Divides information into relevant parts for presentation
- Uses correct spelling, grammar, and punctuation
- Presents the information in a way that is clearly organized and easy to follow
- Shows an understanding of the topic and related concepts
- Fulfills all the requirements of the assignment

Women's Movements

The first wave of the women's movement coincided with **suffrage** campaigns in Europe and the United States, starting in the mid- to late 19th century. The right to vote is a fundamental right for citizens of a democracy. Eventually, the first-wave movement was successful in gaining the right to vote for women. An amendment to the Constitution in 1920 gave women nationwide the right to vote in the United States. Full voting rights for women was achieved in 1928 in Great Britain and 1944 in France.

The second wave of the women's movement developed in the 1960s. This second wave was part of a larger cycle of global social movements, such as independence movements in **developing countries** and the civil rights movement in the United States. The second wave focused, to a large extent, on issues related to equal access to employment and education.

The third wave of the women's movement emerged in the 1980s and 1990s. It drew attention to the concerns of women in marginalized groups. They included women outside the Western

In 1911, almost a decade before the 19th Amendment guaranteed women's suffrage throughout the United States, women in California campaigned for and won the right to vote in state elections.

world, women in the **Global South** and former European colonies, women of color, and working-class women in Western democracies. Such women face very different barriers of economic exploitation and political oppression than those of the white middle-class women from the earlier women's movements. The third-wave movement recognized the diversity of women's conditions, voices, and experiences.

Voting Rights around the World

Women in most **developed countries** did not have the right to vote until the early to mid-20th century. New Zealand was the first country to give women the right to vote at the national level, in 1893. In the United States, suffragists were not only mocked and ridiculed, but they also risked assault and arrest, as was the case with the famous women's rights advocate Susan B. Anthony, who was arrested in 1872 for attempting to vote in that year's presidential election.

At the end of World War I, which lasted from 1914 to 1918, several countries, including Germany, gave women the right to vote. Other nations in Europe, such as Greece, adopted the right to vote for women well after World War II, which ended in 1945. Similar movements can be seen during the 1930s and 1940s in Latin American countries such as Brazil and Argentina. Asian countries such as China and Japan gave women the right to vote in the mid-20th century. In Africa in the late 1950s and 1960s, women obtained the right to vote along with men as former European colonies gained independence. In the Middle East, many countries passed laws after World War II providing for universal suffrage for men and women.

When Women Gained the Right to Vote in Selected Countries

Women in many nations gained the right to participate in their country's elections during the early or mid-20th century. In some countries, universal suffrage for women came much later.

Year	Country
1906	Finland
1913	Norway
1915	Denmark
1918	Russia
1919	Netherlands
1921	Sweden
1928	Ireland
1931	Spain
1934	Turkey
1945	Italy
1947	Japan
1949	China
1950	India
1954	Colombia
1957	Zimbabwe
1962	Algeria
1963	Iran
1964	Libya
1971	Switzerland
1972	Bangladesh
1976	Portugal
1988	Namibia
1990	Samoa
1994	South Africa
2005	Kuwait
2006	United Arab Emirates
2015	Saudi Arabia

ACTIVITIES

Document

A flyer listing reasons for a constitutional amendment, printed by the National American Woman Suffrage Association, July 1918.

Evaluate the arguments used by suffragists to support their claim for women's voting rights.

1. Why was women's suffrage defined as "inevitable"? Which countries are used as an example? Why would their example be effective in convincing the U.S. government to approve voting rights for women? Explain your answer.
2. Why did the suffragists believe that "'A 100 per cent American' Republic cannot logically deny to its women the political liberty that monarchies have extended"?
3. In your opinion, how might these arguments have been received by opponents of women's suffrage? What arguments could have they used to rebut the suffragists' position? Formulate some hypotheses.

RUBRIC

Analyzing Bias in a Video

Students will analyze the bias that exists in a video about an issue facing workers, and how that bias shapes the opinions presented in the video. An exemplary analysis of bias in a video will meet the following criteria.

- Identifies the main points presented in the video
- Offers an in-depth interpretation of the video
- Differentiates between facts and opinions
- Identifies and presents information about the writer
- Assesses the writer's reliability
- Determines the goals of the video
- Considers and assesses the writer's perspective
- Determines the writer's intended audience
- Describes the context in which the video was created, and analyzes how this context might have shaped the opinions expressed in the video
- Infers what political or societal influences might have shaped the opinions presented in the video
- Determines whether the writer had first-hand knowledge of the topic or event, or whether he or she is reporting as a secondary source
- Determines the bias in the video
- Explores other sources related to the topic of the video to compare perspectives and facts

Feminism and Feminists

Feminism can be defined as the belief in the social, political, and economic equality of women and men. Feminism also refers to the women's movements organized around that belief. Feminist concepts and goals may vary by culture and time, but the common thread to all feminist perspectives and movements is the focus on improving **gender rights** and gender equality.

Islamic Feminism

The term *Islamic feminism* was coined by **expatriate** Iranian feminists in the early 1990s to describe a new discussion among women practicing their religion in the Islamic Republic of Iran. They published their ideas about the role of women in society in a magazine called *Zanan* (Women). Islamic feminism considers the place of women in Islam and the Koran. It also seeks rights and justice within the framework of gender equality. As such, Islamic feminism engages Islamic **theology**, in terms of both its text and its traditions.

The Western world sometimes highlights Muslim women's issues by focusing on whether or not women should be allowed to wear the veil in public. For example, the *hijab*, or head scarf, is banned in public schools in France. Islamic feminists question the central definition of equality, or what equality means and how it might be expressed for women in Muslim and non-Muslim societies.

More specifically, feminists argue that gender inequality can be found in all past and present societies and takes the form of patriarchy. *Patriarchy*, which means "rule of the father," refers to a male-dominated society in which women have less power. Patriarchal societies exist throughout the world today to varying degrees. Patriarchy justifies gender inequality by focusing on biological differences between the sexes in order to enforce differential treatment between men and women. This justification is called sexism.

Sexism refers to a system of beliefs, or ideology, that asserts the inferiority of one sex and justifies discrimination based on gender. At the personal level, personal sexism refers to attitudes and behaviors communicated through everyday interaction. At the societal level, institutional sexism refers to a system of policies within institutions, such as education, health, and politics, that creates a hierarchy. In this hierarchy, women are treated unequally compared to men.

Feminism and Gender Inequality

Feminist approaches to the study of gender inequality include the liberal feminist tradition, or mainstream feminism. Other approaches include Marxist feminism and radical feminism. There is also **postcolonial** and global feminism.

Liberal feminism is rooted in the idea that all people are created equal and are entitled to a set of basic rights. Liberal feminists advocate that no one should be denied equality or opportunity because of that person's gender. Thus, from the liberal-feminist perspective, the cause of women's oppression and the inequality between men and women are rooted in a lack of opportunity and in a lack of education for individuals or groups. In this view, the solution for change is for women to gain access to opportunities through the institutions of education and economics.

The women's movements inspired by this perspective have worked for the right to vote, to gain an education, to own property, to be employed, and to be free from discrimination in the workplace. The assumption is that once these barriers are removed, the experiences and opportunities for men and women will converge. The result will be equal rights for both women and men.

Marxist feminism traces the oppression of women back to the beginnings of private property. According to this perspective, the inferior social position of women is linked to the social organization of the economic order, particularly class-based capitalism. Therefore, what distinguishes this approach is its focus on class inequality as the primary source of oppression for women.

Marxist feminism argues that, in the workforce, women are used as cheap, or underpaid, labor and are segregated to low-paid jobs and positions. It also argues that, in the home, women are free, or unpaid, labor, providing services such as cooking and cleaning. The focus of Marxist feminism is on structural and economic factors of oppression, as opposed to the

ACTIVITIES

Video

Women's History Month: Faces of Feminism

Debate what feminism is by analyzing the views of these female writers.

1. Do you agree with the comparison between democracy and feminism? In your opinion, why do advances made in democracy and feminism both "tend to evaporate when we stop fighting"? Support your answer.
2. Why do some people think that feminism is "against men"? Do you agree with this vision? Why do you agree? Why do you disagree?
3. What is feminism, according to the speakers? How do you define "feminism"? Explain your answers.

Title IX and Equality in Sports

Sports is an area in which social norms historically impacted female students in the United States. Before 1972, no federal law prevented U.S. schools from operating athletic programs that discriminated against female participation. In many schools, the male athletic programs were much better funded, included more sports, and had better facilities and equipment than programs for female students. Then, Congress passed legislation known as the Education Amendments of 1972. A section of this legislation, Title IX, required every educational institution receiving financial assistance from the U.S. Department of Education (DOE) to offer male and female students equal opportunities to play sports. Almost all U.S. schools receive some DOE funding and were impacted by the new law. Title IX changed many of the rules and practices governing school athletic programs. For female students, sports scholarships, access to coaching, the quality and quantity of sports equipment, and time for games and practices all dramatically increased. According to NOW, one in 27 U.S. female high-school students played varsity-level sports before 1972. Today, that proportion has increased more than tenfold, to one in every 2.5 female students.

individual-opportunities approach advocated by liberal feminism.

Radical feminism argues that men directly benefit from the subordination of women. It also argues that men's superior position in many societies is based on ensuring women's inferiority. Thus, in this view, patriarchy and sexism are at the core of oppression against women. The overall assessment of radical feminists is that in order to challenge the existing status quo of gender inequality, society needs to question the entire ideology behind patriarchy.

Postcolonial and global feminism explicitly acknowledges that gender intersects with race and class. It also intersects with issues of colonization and the exploitation and oppression of women worldwide. The focus overall is on identifying and denouncing the negative effects of patriarchy on the condition of women of color, working-class women, and women of the Global South.

Dig Deeper

The United Nations Development Programme publishes an annual report that covers gender equality around the world. Explore this report online. What are the biggest issues for women? Write an essay outlining one or two of these issues and possible solutions.

Clara Zetkin, a German Marxist feminist who lived from 1857 to 1933, organized the first International Women's Day in 1911. Now held every year on March 8, International Women's Day celebrates women's achievements and promotes gender equality.

ACTIVITIES

Weblink

History of International Women's Day

Analyze the history of International Women's Day.

1. How has the relationship between International Women's Day and politics evolved over time? Why was this celebration closely linked to specific political messages in the past? Is it still associated with political messages nowadays? Why or why not?
2. Were the political links between International Women's Day and socialism or communism the only reasons for which the United States did not celebrate it between 1913 and 1975? What other reasons could have contributed to United States' decision to disregard the International Women's Day celebrations? Formulate some hypotheses.

RUBRIC

Analyzing a Primary Source

Students will complete a thorough analysis of a primary source. An exemplary analysis will meet the following criteria.

- Identifies the creator of the source
- Explains what medium was used to create the primary source
- Describes why the source qualifies as a primary one
- Explores any literary devices used in the source
- Identifies the intended audience for the source
- Relates the creator's goals in creating the source
- Illustrates knowledge of the period and location in which the source was created
- Distinguishes between facts and opinions found in the source
- Assesses the reliability of the source's creator
- Compares the source with similar documents
- Cites additional sources used in the analysis
- Presents information in a clear, concise manner
- Uses correct spelling, grammar, and punctuation

CHAPTER 3

A large majority of children in the United States are part of two-parent households. About one-fourth of children live only with their mother, and one in 25 lives only with his or her father.

Gender Equality and Domestic Life

As most societies throughout the world are based on patriarchy, women have not always had equal standing with men within the family. In the United States, for example, before the mid-1800s, women did not have any legal existence independent of their husbands. The 1839 Married Women's Property Acts made it possible, in the U.S. states that adopted such legislation, for married women to own and control property. These laws also allowed married women to participate in contracts and lawsuits, inherit independently of their husbands, write their own wills, and work for a salary. In most Western societies, women eventually acquired legal access to property ownership, inheritance, and other rights. However, women worldwide still experience barriers to gaining property rights and acquiring an independent legal status.

Another legal rights issue for women is the law regarding family names and married names. The law in Western societies does not require women to take a spouse's name when they marry, although most women do. In countries such as South Korea and Italy, however, women keep their maiden name. The maiden name represents the heritage of their own family, which they wish to continue.

About 40 Percent
Portion of U.S. households in which women are the primary financial provider.

100%
Percentage of children in Finland under the age of 7 who have the legal right to access to preschool programs, regardless of family income.

1993
Year the U.S. Congress passed the Family and Medical Leave Act.

ACTIVITIES

Document

Mississippi Married Women's Property Law (1939)
Analyze the first married women's property act adopted in the United States.

1. How did the Act enable women to own and control property? In your opinion, were its measures effective in enabling women to own and control property? Why or why not?
2. How have women's ownership rights evolved since the establishment of this act? What were the factors that lead to the evolution of these rights over time? Formulate some hypotheses.

First Hand

'I Didn't Want to Lose My Identity': 16,000 Readers Reflect on Their Surname
Analyze the position of different women about keeping or changing their surnames when they married.

1. What are the main arguments of women who chose to change their surnames and those of women who chose to keep their surnames? Are these arguments valid? Do these arguments differ based on the geographical origin of these women? Explain your answers.
2. If you were a married woman, would you change your surname? Why or why not?

Marriage and Family

The term *sexual division of labor* refers to the process through which tasks are assigned on the basis of gender. In the case of domestic labor, or housework, it refers to the way tasks required to run and maintain a household are distributed between the sexes. Depending on the society and country, these tasks may include childcare, food shopping, cooking, cleaning, laundry, yard work, household maintenance, financial accounting, and car maintenance. At least some of these tasks are traditionally carried out according to gender.

Industrialization, which began in the 18th century, has altered family life in Western societies. Before industrialization, agriculture was the means of subsistence for most families. Farms were the place of both work and home, and everyone in the household contributed their labor without a gender divide. Industrialization altered this arrangement for men and women.

With the creation of factories, production of goods moved out of the home. This physical separation of work and family inspired the creation of two distinct domains, each with different gender roles and expectations. Traditional men's roles were organized

During the 19th century, in European cities such as Glasgow, Scotland, industry flourished and provided opportunities for work outside the home, mostly for men.

around the status of worker outside the home, or paid labor, while women were often assigned the traditional role of stay-at-home parent, or unpaid labor.

Today, in most Western and industrialized societies, although women work outside the home, they remain responsible for the vast majority of the housework. The average woman with a paid job works an extra four 24-hour days per year, compared to her spouse, doing housework and family caretaking. Social scientists call this the second shift. The size of the second shift is down from about three decades ago, when the average mother with a paid job worked an extra month of 24-hour days.

The Division of Labor in Global Perspective

The separation of the domestic sphere, or family life, from the public sphere, or paid work, is called the doctrine of the separate spheres. This ideology developed in Western societies. Great global variation exists in the types of tasks people need to do and in the ways in which gender is used to divide responsibility for those tasks.

In the Lahu ethnic group in southwest China, people believe that women and men share equal responsibility for child rearing and other tasks a household must accomplish together. The husband is expected to take over much of his wife's work during her pregnancy, and he participates in the pregnancy by monitoring his wife's experiences and bodily changes. Lahu parents take their infants and children with them into the fields to work, and in all facets of their life, they share responsibility for the care of their children, including holding the babies during the night to keep them from crying.

ACTIVITIES

Weblink

Women and the Early Industrial Revolution in the United States

Evaluate the role of American women in the early industrial revolution.

1. How did the social and economic changes caused by the industrial revolution influence women's lives? Support your answer with examples.
2. In your opinion, what does the author mean when he says that factory employment provided women with "a collective experience that supported their participation in the world of broader social reform"? Would women's rights and other civil rights have evolved differently, had women not had a role in the early industrial revolution? Why? How could have they evolved? Formulate some hypotheses.

The size of the gender gap varies. For example, only about one-half of couples in Japan share household duties. However, about 93 percent of couples in the United States and 87 percent of couples in South Korea share household tasks. In the United States, the closer men's earnings are to women's, the more housework men do. Interestingly, however, men who are economically dependent on their wives tend to do less housework than other men.

Work–Family Conflict

In industrialized societies, the family and work spheres are often in conflict with one another. This work–family conflict is a result of the tension that people confront between job demands and home demands. Employed women and men also face conflict when they try to distribute household tasks fairly.

In many of the world's countries, working people are responsible for

Although many couples in Germany share housework, one study found that German women spent twice as much time as men on household chores and childcare.

caring for others in addition to their children, such as elderly parents or spouses. Studies show that employed women tend to experience more stress than men with regard to caring for other family members, as they are more likely than men to take on greater family responsibilities. However, a growing number of men, especially younger men, spend significantly more time with children than their counterparts did a few decades ago.

Some countries have addressed the work–family conflict by helping workers accommodate their dual responsibilities. Western European countries provide paid parental leave to working parents during a child's early years. These nations also support quality out-of-home care for children, such as child-care centers and preschools. Paid parental leave is now common among Western European nations, including France, Germany, Italy, Great Britain, Norway, and Portugal.

In the United States, the Family and Medical Leave Act (FMLA) requires employers to allow certain workers up to 12 workweeks of unpaid leave for a pregnancy, adoption, or family medical emergency. Employers covered by this law must also maintain the health-insurance benefits of eligible workers during the unpaid leave. FMLA does not require that employers offer any paid parental leave. Public agencies and schools must follow FMLA rules. However, the rules apply only to private employers that have 50 or more employees for at least 20 workweeks per year. Companies with fewer employees do not even have to offer workers unpaid leave without risk of job loss.

In 2017, the United States was one of only eight United Nations (UN) member states without any national program

On average, among married American caregivers who are age 75 or older, both sexes provide equal amounts of care.

ACTIVITIES

Video

Confessions of Moms Around the World

Analyze the views of work-family conflict and the solutions adopted by women around the world.

1. How does maternity leave differ around the world? How does maternity leave availability influence the lives of women with children around the world? Are these differences related only to the duration of the maternity leave? What are the other possible reasons behind these differences?
2. Are cultural differences playing a role in improving or worsening the work-family conflict around the world? If yes, what role do they play? If no, why are they not playing a role?
3. What are the challenges faced by women with children? Are these challenges similar around the world, or are they specific to a country? Why or why not?

for paid parental leave. Scholars argue that there are cultural and ideological reasons why the United States lags behind other countries. For one thing, with their high value on individualism, Americans see childbearing and child-care duties as a private matter rather than a public concern. Additionally, the workplace culture in the United States sees work–family programs as a hindrance to business and to workers' productivity and commitment. However, an increasing number of employers in the United States have taken on more responsibility for implementing work–family balance programs.

Parental Leave around the World

The average parental leave in the 35 developed countries that are members of the Organisation for Economic Co-operation and Development (OECD) is 10 months. Paid parental leave for use by both mothers and fathers is now available in 23 OECD countries. Parental leave for fathers allows them to take a greater share of the childcare responsibilities. In this way, parental leave can help women's advancement in the workplace. Many developing countries also support paid parental leave. For example, Jamaica provides 8 weeks at the minimum wage, while Nicaragua provides 12 weeks at 60 percent of the worker's wage. Benin provides full pay for 14 weeks.

Women's Rights and Health

Reproductive rights can be defined as the legal rights and freedoms related to reproduction and reproductive health. Around the world, countries take different approaches to the laws that affect reproduction. These laws are often rooted in cultural traditions and religious beliefs. Legislation regarding reproductive health directly affects women and their babies. The larger society also has a stake in the health and wellness of women and the future citizens to whom they give birth.

Global reproductive health initiatives include the right to access health care services that support healthy pregnancies, safe childbirth, and the birth of healthy infants. In recent decades, such initiatives have had a positive impact. Between 1990 and 2016, global infant mortality dropped from 65 to 31 deaths per 1,000 live births.

Dig Deeper

Interview a family or a couple about their division of labor in the household. Present a list of household tasks, and ask your respondents to identify tasks they do on a regular basis and indicate what their ideal division of labor would be. Write a report describing your findings and analyzing the extent to which gender influences the division of household tasks for the people you interviewed.

African American women are three times as likely to die in pregnancy or childbirth as white Americans. Some maternal health experts have called for better certification of hospitals, to ensure they provide high-quality care, and the expansion of support programs for pregnant women.

ACTIVITIES

Weblink

Paid parental leave elusive 25 years after Family and Medical Leave Act

Analyze the challenges posed by the current formulation of the Family and Medical Leave Act.

1. In your opinion, why does the Family and Medical Leave Act not include freelancers and companies with fewer than 50 employees? Why has it not established any form of income replacement? Formulate some hypotheses.
2. Besides increasing the duration of maternity leave period and establishing income replacement, what other solutions could be adopted to reduce the challenges faced by women after giving birth, and the risk for mental health issues related to inadequate paid leave policies?

CHAPTER 4

Higher education has become an essential tool for increasing one's wages. According to the U.S. Department of Education, women are enrolling in college at higher rates than men, and by 2026, 57 percent of college students will be women.

Gender Equality and the Public Sphere

The sexual division of labor is a fundamental feature of work. All societies delegate tasks in part on the basis of gender, although how big a factor it is varies over time and across countries. For example, farming in many Asian societies is reserved strictly for men, while in many African societies, farming is a livelihood of women. Also, most tailors are male in many parts of the Middle East, North Africa, and India, but the occupation is a largely female one in industrialized countries.

Sex segregation in the workplace refers to the concentration or unequal distribution of women and men into different jobs, occupations, and firms. Sex segregation also refers to situations in which the sexes share the same workplace but do different jobs. This might include a dental office where female dental hygienists work alongside male dentists. While most dental hygienists in the United States are women, the portion of female dentists has risen in recent decades to more than 30 percent of the profession.

In the United States, female-dominated occupations include preschool and kindergarten teachers, speech-language pathologists, administrative assistants, paralegals and legal

14%
Portion of American women ages 25 to 64 with advanced degrees, compared with 12 percent of men.

More Than One-half
Portion of working-age women in the United States who were either employed or looking for work.

2%
Portion of France's largest firms in which the highest-level executive is a woman.

ACTIVITIES

Weblink

Why Men are the New College Minority

Analyze the reasons for and possible solutions to low numbers of men enrolling in college education.

1. What factors contribute to the low rate of men pursuing college education compared to women? Are contemporary gender norms and expectations contributing to this low rate? Why or why not?
2. What measures are colleges implementing to attract more men? Do you consider these solutions effective? Why or why not? What other measures could be adopted to achieve the same objective?
3. Why are higher numbers of women enrolling in college considered a problem that needs a solution? Formulate some hypotheses.

RUBRIC

Holding a Classroom Debate

Students will form groups and prepare arguments for a debate on a controversial issue. Exemplary performance in a debate will meet the following criteria.

- Demonstrates in-depth understanding of the topic and related information
- Presents strong, logical, and convincing arguments
- Communicates in a clear and confident manner
- Uses clear vocal inflection and tone
- Uses a reasonable rate of vocal delivery
- Uses respectful and appropriate language and body language
- Delivers arguments, supporting evidence, and counterevidence in an engaging and persuasive manner
- Supports each major point of an argument with several relevant and detailed facts and examples
- Connects all arguments to the overall topic in a clear, concise, and organized manner
- Presents clear, thorough, and accurate information throughout the debate
- Identifies any weakness in the opposing team's arguments
- Presents counterarguments confidently, showing preparation for this component prior to the debate
- Presents strong and persuasive arguments throughout the debate
- Summarizes the arguments in the closing statement

assistants, and housekeeping cleaners. Only about 6 percent of childcare workers in the United States are male. Predominantly male occupations include airline pilots, auto mechanics, engineers, and corporate chief executives. However, many occupations have changed their gender label over time. Librarian, clerical worker, and bank teller used to be mainly male occupations, for example, but now women occupy a majority of these positions.

This type of occupational segregation is present in all religious, social, political, and economic systems. Women tend to be limited to fewer occupations than men, as well as to occupations that carry less income, less authority, and less prestige. Occupations that seem to require nurturing such as nurse or child-care worker sometimes correspond to some of the stereotypes about women.

Occupational Segregation around the World

The Middle East and North Africa have the highest levels of occupational segregation, while countries in the Asia-Pacific region have the lowest. In countries in Asia, occupational segregation is qualitatively different. Women are able to obtain jobs in a wider range of occupations, and more women have jobs in the private sector, particularly in larger better-paying companies in which they may be promoted to higher ranks. Additionally, some countries, such as China, have a greater commitment to gender equity through government policies. In contrast, countries in the Middle East and North Africa tend to have a higher level of gender inequality. In these countries, women experience

Occupational segregation exists for workers in various fields. In the United States, only 2.5 percent of preschool teachers are male.

more cultural barriers to accessing various occupations. Among the OECD countries, the United States and Canada have the lowest levels of gender segregation.

Gender Wage Gap

The wage gap between men and women is the disparity in their earnings for their work, usually measured by the ratio of women's to men's median earnings. The gender wage gap is a global pattern. However, it has varied across time and place, as well as varying in size.

The earnings ratio is lowest in the North African and the Middle Eastern countries of Libya, Iraq, Saudi Arabia, Bahrain, the United Arab Emirates, Oman, and Qatar. In these nations, employed women earn less than 20 percent of men's earnings. The highest earnings ratios can be found in Sweden, Cambodia, and Tanzania, where women earn between 80 and 90 percent of men's earnings. High earnings ratios in Sweden can be explained by the fact that Sweden and other Scandinavian countries have a centralized wage-setting mechanism for industries and occupations. Cambodia and Tanzania have a small gender wage gap because men's earnings in most occupations are low and therefore close to that of women.

In the United States, the gender wage gap is smaller than in the past, but it persists. For every dollar a man earns, a woman earns about 83 cents. For workers between the ages of 25 and 34, the wage gap is smaller, with a difference of only 10 cents. The U.S. wage gap is more pronounced for women of color. Additionally, women earn less in almost every occupation, including those containing high percentages of women, such as nursing. Social scientists attribute the U.S. wage gap to several factors, including discrimination, gender stereotypes, employers' pay practices, and the devaluation of women's work. Some employers discriminate against women by paying them less than men on the

Gender Wage Gap in the United States

The gender pay gap for full-time or part-time U.S. workers ages 16 and older has decreased since 1980. However, in 2016, the median hourly wage of men was still $3.23 greater than that of women. More women in better-paid occupations, such as management jobs, have helped narrow the gender wage gap.

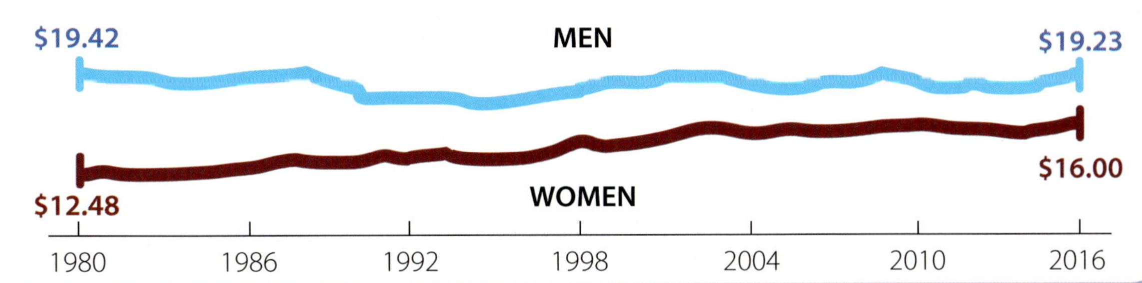

ACTIVITIES

Document

Issue Brief. Women's Earnings and the Wage Gap

Read the Women's Bureau of U.S. Department of Labor report and evaluate the status of women's earnings and the wage gap in the United States by reading the Women's Bureau of the U.S. Department of Labor report.

1. Why are workers aged 55 to 64 more affected by earning disparity? Formulate some hypotheses.
2. Why do women who are members of unions or covered by union contracts have higher earnings and greater access to pensions and health insurance? Discuss some possible reasons.

Weblink

The Jobs Most Segregated by Gender and Race

Analyze the data about sex and race segregation in different professional fields.

1. What are the main reasons for sex and race segregation in the workplace? Do these two forms of segregation stem from the same reasons? Why or why not?
2. In your opinion, why are the specific occupations listed the ones mostly affected by sex segregation in the workplace? Debate the possible causes of sex segregation in these professional fields.

basis of generalizations about women and men as groups.

The belief that men require higher pay because they support their families is still present in the United States. That type of thinking can affect women's wages negatively. Hiring, placement, and promotion decisions can also be influenced by discrimination. Finally, in the United States, types of jobs filled principally by women tend to be devalued, regardless of what those jobs entail, simply because women do them. Consequently, a higher value, in terms of wage setting, is placed on jobs and activities associated with men.

Worldwide, factors such as sex segregation, **gender discrimination**, occupational structures, and cultural beliefs can explain the persistence of the wage gap. Even when education, experience, and seniority are equal, men still out-earn women. In a number of Western countries, women have been slowly catching up with men's earnings.

Gender Discrimination and the Glass Ceiling

Discrimination refers to the unequal treatment of individuals due to personal characteristics unrelated to their performance. Around the world and throughout history, employers have openly discriminated on the basis of gender. In most Western democracies and other countries in the world, legislation and government policies have outlawed employment discrimination on the basis of gender. However, despite progress, patterns of gender discrimination worldwide still persist in a variety of more covert, less obvious ways.

Gender discrimination can be based on gender stereotypes that shape the views of employers about prospective workers. Employers also often discriminate against women out of deference to the prejudices of their customers or workers. In addition, gender discrimination includes sexual harassment. Women are much more likely than men to suffer this kind of harassment in the workplace. Victims of such harassment might feel they have to resign or request a transfer. Sometimes, women may lose their jobs or be pressured to resign after they report inappropriate conduct by supervisors or coworkers.

Another form of gender discrimination is the glass ceiling. This is a theoretical barrier that limits women's upward mobility. The term refers to the fact that women are still far less likely than men to occupy positions that involve exercising authority and power over people and resources.

In general, the higher the level of authority in an organization, the less likely women are to be represented. In particular, women are underrepresented in top jobs in the professions, the military, and unions. Among the **Fortune 500** companies, there were 23 women chief executive officers (CEOs) in May 2018, which represents about 5 percent of all CEOs in the Fortune 500. Only two of the female CEOs were women of color. The most significant explanations for these inequalities in promotions are the segregation of women in certain jobs in an organization, a lack of mentoring programs for women, and outdated personnel practices.

Equality and the Media

In most media sources, including movies, comic books, and popular music, sex-role behavior is portrayed in a highly stereotyped fashion. The portrayal of women on prime-time television remains stereotypical. For example, male characters are more likely than female ones to be shown working outside the home. Female characters express emotions much more easily and are significantly more likely to use charm to get what they want than are male characters.

Analysis of the portrayal of women in advertising, fashion, television, music videos, and films reveals a double-edged stereotype. Women are presented as the perfect wife, mother, or career woman, or as people to be valued based on their physical appearance. The **objectification** of women does not further gender equality.

Dig Deeper

Find a few common personal care products in the drugstore, on television, or online. Is the packaging, description, and advertising geared to men, women, or both? Analyze the different messages the product manufacturers present and what these messages convey about men and women.

ACTIVITIES

Video

The Glass Ceiling Is Misleading

Analyze the concept of the glass ceiling and its limits.

1. Why does the speaker consider the glass ceiling "not a good metaphor"? Do you agree with the reasons she offers to justify her opinion? Why or why not?
2. What is your personal opinion of the glass ceiling metaphor? What other metaphors could be used to better define the "glass ceiling phenomenon"? Propose some possible alternatives.

The Glass Ceiling Worldwide

The glass ceiling phenomenon affects women worldwide. In Norway, in recognition of the underrepresentation of women on company boards of directors, the legislature established, in 2003, minimum quotas for the number of female board members. The goal was to reach a 40 percent representation by 2008, which was accomplished. However, many of Norway's biggest companies have failed to meet the quota, and a handful still have no women on their boards.

RUBRIC

Analyzing a Video

Students will watch a video and write an analysis. An exemplary video analysis will meet the following criteria.

- Identifies the purpose of the video
- Identifies the intended audience of the video
- Identifies the video as a primary or secondary source
- Discusses the historical and social context of the video
- Describes how the content of the video is presented
- Summarizes the information and opinions presented in the video
- Evaluates the quality of the content presented in the video
- Assesses the effectiveness of the video
- Determines whether the images and graphics used in the video relate to the content
- Determines whether the video is easy to follow and understand
- Gives the analysis a clear and consistent purpose
- Organizes the analysis in a logical, effective manner
- Presents a strong, clear argument about the video
- Provides strong and accurate details to support the argument about the video
- Considers other perspectives on the purpose and effectiveness of the video
- Cites all sources used in the analysis
- Uses correct spelling, grammar, and punctuation

CHAPTER 5

On International Women's Day in 2018, demonstrators in Seoul, South Korea, showed their support for the #MeToo movement.

Future Challenges

A 2001 United Nations report noted that, in many nations, women are denied equal pay, harassed at work, or dismissed from their jobs because they were pregnant. Women who do assert or defend their rights are routinely ignored or, worse, punished for their protest. The lack of widespread support, at least until quite recently, for changes related to job-site sexual harassment and equal-pay-for-equal-work stands in sharp contrast to the global attention given to some other challenging issues that negatively impact women more than men. While efforts to end domestic violence, **human trafficking**, and war crimes continue to face difficulties, these issues have for years attracted wider condemnation and increased support for change.

#MeToo and Time's Up are empowerment movements that use social media campaigns to attract attention to a lack of progress on feminist issues, such as workplace harassment and pay equity. Founded in 2006 and 2018, respectively, #MeToo and Time's Up started in the United States before earning global support. Both movements give women and men a platform to talk publicly about the struggle for equal treatment in the workplace, as well as justice in the legal system for victims of assault or other illegal actions. #MeToo and Time's Up also promote awareness of how disadvantaged women and women of color are at greater risk of harassment, violence, and workplace discrimination. The Time's Up organization actively raises money to cover the legal fees of women who cannot afford to pursue legal redress for discriminatory workplace practices.

Six
Total number of female U.S. state governors in early 2018.

1851
Year Elizabeth Blackwell, the first woman to graduate from a U.S. medical school, was denied a position at any New York City hospital.

15%
Portion of U.S. Army personnel in 2017 who were women.

ACTIVITIES

Video

#MeToo founder Tarana Burke: "A hashtag is not a movement."
Assess the effects of media coverage on the #MeToo movement.

1. What does Tarana Burke mean by the statement, "a hashtag is not a movement"? How has the involvement of people on the internet helped the movement grow? How has this involvement limited the movement's success? Explain your answer.
2. Do you agree with Tarana Burke's assessment of journalism? Why or why not? In your opinion, how does journalism, and more generally media, influence the public perception of the most recent feminist movements? Defend your opinion.

Weblink

TIME'S UP
Evaluate the development and the purposes of the Time's Up organization.

1. In what context did the organization develop? In your opinion, why did this organization develop only in 2018? Formulate some hypotheses.
2. What are the main goals of the organization? How does the organization propose to achieve these goals? Do you believe these are effective ways to achieve these aims? What other action could be taken to achieve them?

Women in Politics

Despite the fact that political elites, or small groups of people in high-level positions of power and responsibility in government, are mostly men, scholars have found that women have played a significant role in politics historically. Women's social movements include peace movements and equal rights campaigns. Women were involved in the civil rights movement of the 1950s and 1960s in the United States. They played key roles in the overthrow of the aristocracy in 18th-century France and in the riots that helped spark the Russian Revolution in the early 20th century.

In 2017, 15 countries had female heads of state or heads of government. These countries included Switzerland, Norway, Poland, Lithuania, Estonia, New Zealand, Malta, Namibia, Bangladesh, and Germany. However, such countries represented less than 10 percent of all United Nation members. Additionally, in national legislatures, women held less than one-fourth of all seats worldwide. Great Britain and Canada, two established democracies, had 33 percent and 26 percent women, respectively, present in their national legislatures. A number of countries had higher percentages, including Sweden, with 44 percent, South Africa, with 42 percent, and Cuba, with 49 percent. In the United States, 20 percent of members of Congress were women, or 107 out of 535 total members. Rwanda and Bolivia were the only countries in which the portion of women in national legislatures exceeded 50 percent, at 61 percent and 53 percent, respectively.

To remedy this situation, some countries have adopted quotas for female

Olympe de Gouges

In France, playwright and political activist Olympe de Gouges, as well as other women in her social circle, actively participated in the 1789 French Revolution. Olympe de Gouges advocated for a change of political institutions from **absolute monarchy** to a more equitable system, particularly for women. In 1791, she wrote the *Declaration of the Rights of Woman and the Female Citizen*, demanding that French women be given the same rights as men. She also advocated against slavery in French colonies and opposed capital punishment.

representatives. Governments may set aside a certain percentage of legislative seats for women, from 14 percent to 30 percent. Some political parties have pledged that 20 percent to 40 percent of their candidates will be women.

Women in Business

In the past, women often got their start in business when they assumed control of a family-owned enterprise, such as a farm, shop, or service business, after the death of the family's male leader. About 1,400 years ago, Khadijah, a wife of Muhammad, the founder of Islam, took over her father's trading business after he died. In the 1700s, following the death of her mother and her father's return to Great Britain, Eliza Lucas Pinckney operated her father's plantations in South Carolina, eventually earning a reputation for exporting high-quality dye for the textile industry. In 1963, Katharine Graham became publisher of the *Washington Post*, a newspaper that had been purchased by her father. This family connection made her the first woman publisher of a major American newspaper.

Women working in businesses not linked to their families have had much more difficulty reaching executive positions, although there have been exceptions. In the early 20th century, Elizabeth Arden in the United States and Coco Chanel in France started and ran highly successful businesses related to women's cosmetics and fashion. In 2017, American businesses with women in the top leadership role included PepsiCo, International Business Machines, Kraft Foods, General Dynamics, and General Motors.

Nevertheless, women hold a far smaller percentage of executive positions than the 50 percent that they make up of all U.S. workers. Moreover, research shows that almost 50 percent of male workers surveyed believe women are "well represented" at the executive level, even in companies where only one in 10 senior staff positions is held by a woman. The same misperception is seen when women are asked the same type of question. One-third of female respondents think women are well represented in firms in which only one in 10 senior positions is filled by a woman.

Women in Science

Data from the U.S. Department of Commerce show that women are significantly underrepresented in STEM jobs. Positions in the STEM sector tend to be held by college-educated workers. Compared to men, women hold fewer STEM college degrees. Even when they have a STEM-related degree, women are less likely than their male counterparts to work in a STEM job.

A lack of female role models and gender stereotyping in hiring practices are two of the main challenges. Efforts to boost the number of women in STEM occupations are based on rising demand for STEM workers, as well as on the goals of fairness and equal opportunity. STEM careers can also be a pathway to greater financial security for women, since research indicates that women in STEM jobs

ACTIVITIES

Document

Declaration of the Rights of Woman, 1791

Analyze the text of the Declaration of the Rights of Woman written by Olympe de Gouges in 1791.

1. Why did Olympe de Gouges state that "ignorance, neglect, or contempt for the rights of woman are the sole causes of public misfortunes and governmental corruption"? Why does she affirm that social distinction between man and woman "may be based only on common utility"? Formulate some hypotheses.
2. What idea of equality between men and women does this text convey? Is it similar to or different from the idea of equality we have today? Has this idea evolved over time? How has it evolved? If you do not think it has evolved, why has it remained the same?

typically earn about one-third more than women in comparable non-STEM positions. Besides school-based efforts to encourage female students' interest in STEM, other initiatives include science and math camp programs that are equally welcoming to students of both genders.

Women in the Military

Throughout the world and in all periods of history, it is largely men who have commanded and served in military forces. Today, the national armed forces in almost all countries are still principally male institutions. However, throughout history and around the world, women have participated in the armed forces in different capacities. Moreover, in recent years, many countries have increased opportunities for women in the military.

In some countries, women are included in the military through auxiliary roles and noncombat active roles, and not always at all ranks or in all units. Industrialized societies have varying policies regarding the involvement of women in the military and the extent of their participation in national armed services, especially combatant roles in armed conflicts. Some nations, including Canada and Israel, allow women to participate in frontline combat roles, although they are still underrepresented in these positions. European nations have various regulations that limit the extent of women's participation in combat units.

Women Leaders in the United States

A number of prominent Americans in public life, business, science, and the military have been women. These leaders have improved equity for women in the workplace, created jobs for American workers, advanced scientific understanding of the universe, and defended the nation.

Ruth Bader Ginsburg, who joined the U.S. Supreme Court in 1993, pioneered the concept of gender equality in the law.

Mary Barra was selected to lead one of the three largest American motor-vehicle manufacturing companies.

Vera Rubin, a groundbreaking astronomer, discovered evidence for the existence of dark matter.

Ann Dunwoody served as a four-star general in the U.S. Army, becoming the first woman to hold that rank.

In addition, when women are allowed in combat units, they are not necessarily permitted to participate in direct combat within those units and instead may be limited to other roles. Pakistan is the only Islamic country where women serve in combat units and are appointed to high ranks in the military.

In the United States, until recently, women were restricted to serving in noncombat units. However, since 2015, the U.S. armed forces have included women in all types of units. As in other countries where this move has occurred or is being considered, the widespread integration of female soldiers into military roles is hampered by issues of female safety.

In 2017, almost 7,000 members of the U.S. military reported that they were victims of sexual assault. More than 80 percent of the reports were filed by women. The actual incidence of assault is likely much higher. The U.S. Defense Department has estimated that about one-third of assaults are reported. Sexual harassment and assault within the military may be underreported because victims fear ostracism or retaliation if they come forward. In addition, some victims do not report assault or harassment because they believe their accusations will not be seriously investigated. U.S. military leaders are working to implement programs intended to address these issues.

ACTIVITIES

More

Women Leaders in the United States

Compare and contrast the careers of these four American women leaders.

1. What do these women have in common? How do their experiences differ? How did their gender influence their careers? Support your answers with examples.
2. Could these women's experiences be considered exceptional? Why or why not? Would their careers develop in the same way, had they started their professional lives today? Explain your answer.

Since the mid-1970s, the portion of U.S. military enlisted personnel who are women has increased eightfold, from 2 percent to 16 percent.

RUBRIC

Researching for a Writing Assignment

Students will complete a thorough research process to prepare for a writing assignment and organize their research in a logical manner that supports their writing. An exemplary research process will meet the following criteria.

- Creates a goal for the research, based on the topic and working thesis
- Creates specific, thoughtful, and inventive research questions that are relevant to the topic of the writing assignment
- Produces a list of categories, key words, and related ideas to effectively assist in researching
- Uses high-quality sources that pertain to the topic and come in a variety of formats, such as books, journals, primary sources, websites, and databases
- Uses sources that provide balanced research and various perspectives of the topic in question
- Takes notes to highlight the key facts and ideas in order to answer all research questions
- Extracts relevant, detailed information from the sources
- Writes notes in the student's own words
- Organizes the research notes in a clear and concise manner
- Analyzes the information and produces ideas and points to support the working thesis
- Uses an effective and suitable format to present all research
- Properly cites all sources used
- Uses quotations properly and ethically

Halting Violence against Women

The military is not the only institution where women fear violence. Throughout the world and throughout history, physical and sexual assault are among the most prevalent and feared violent crimes against women. Historically and today, slave owners and human traffickers have used assault to subdue female captives, while armies ancient and modern have deliberately employed violence to hurt and to subjugate civilian women.

Growing interest in halting violence against women acknowledges that change can be difficult. Due to social stigma, including fear of abandonment by families, sexual assault tends to be one of the most underreported crimes. Some cultures even support the idea of "honor killing" and call for the death of an assault victim, because of a belief that the assault has brought shame to the victim's family. Around the world, nonreporting of sexual assault is also linked to notions that the victim was somehow complicit in the assault. This tendency to blame female victims of violence is sometimes called victim shaming.

Increased awareness of female vulnerability to violence is prompting change. Since 1995, more than 100 countries have conducted at least one survey on the issue of violence against women. While change is slow, these nations are working to address the fact

According to the World Economic Forum, at current rates of improvement, gender equality is more than 200 years away. Young global activists use protests to show their support for closing the gender wage gap, ending gender discrimination, and halting violence against women.

that assault, threats of assault, domestic violence, injury at the hands of someone the woman knows, and virtual threats through social media can all be used to hurt, intimidate, and dominate women. Research shows that in almost all countries where information about violence against women has been available for more than one year, the level of acceptance of violence has diminished among both female and male citizens.

Dig Deeper

Research media coverage of a recent political campaign between a male candidate and a female candidate. What information was shared about each person, including family life, political experience, and appearance? Write an essay analyzing any differences.

ACTIVITIES

Weblink

Global Database on Violence against Women

Explore the database and analyze the trends of violence against women and the solutions adopted around the world.

1. What are the functions of this database? Do you think a database is a useful tool for ending violence against women? Why or why not? What other uses could such a tool have?
2. Choose four countries' profiles and compare and contrast the solutions implemented by each to end violence against women. Are these countries affected by violence against women in a similar way? How do the data available for each country differ? How are they similar? What are the measures taken by each country? In your opinion, are these measures effective? How could each country improve the measures it implements? Formulate some hypotheses.

Equality for All

Concerns about violence against women typically mirror other concerns related to gender-based discrimination. Research shows that women who are non-white and those who are economically disadvantaged tend to be at a higher risk for violence than others. For example, while sexual harassment occurs across industries, it is especially common in low-wage service jobs where women of color represent a relatively high percentage of the workforce. Disability also puts women at higher risk of violence.

Nicole Kidman, UN Development Fund for Women (UNIFEM) goodwill ambassador and Australian actor, led a campaign asking UNIFEM to highlight violence against women. In 2008, she presented 5 million signatures of support to UN Secretary General Ban Ki-moon.

RUBRIC

Creating a Timeline

Students will explore a topic from a historical perspective and create a timeline to present their research. An exemplary timeline will meet the following criteria.

- Includes the most significant events pertaining to the topic
- Includes interesting events
- Uses accurate information for all events, including date, location, and major details
- Orders the events in a chronological sequence
- Describes each event with accurate, vivid, and specific details
- Presents the topic from three or more perspectives
- Inspires the reader to ask thoughtful questions regarding the events and perspectives presented in the timeline
- Uses correct spelling, grammar, and punctuation
- Presents the timeline in a visually attractive and striking manner
- Presents the timeline in a neat and organized manner that is logical and easy to follow
- Uses creativity to present the timeline in an engaging manner
- Effectively communicates historical information relating to the topic
- Supports each event with reliable sources
- Includes a correctly formatted bibliography of all sources used to create the timeline

Timeline

Since the 18th century, global gender equality has often progressed slowly. In the 21st century, women around the world are participating in the political process, closing the gender wage gap, serving in the world's militaries, and fighting for professional equity.

New Zealand becomes the first country to give women the right to vote at the national level.

1791 **1848** **1872** **1893**

French writer Olympe de Gouges publishes the *Declaration of the Rights of Woman and the Female Citizen.*

In Seneca Falls, New York, an assembly of more than 200 people, led by Elizabeth Cady Stanton and Lucretia Mott, launches the U.S. women's suffrage movement.

American suffragist Susan B. Anthony is arrested for attempting to vote in the U.S. presidential election.

The National Organization for Women is founded to promote equal rights for women.

The U.S. federal law called the Family and Medical Leave Act is passed, requiring employers to allow workers up to 12 workweeks of unpaid time off for a pregnancy, adoption, or family medical emergency.

Women in the U.S. military are permitted to serve in combat posts.

1920 | 1966 | 1993 | 2013 | 2015 | 2018

The 19th Amendment to the U.S. Constitution goes into effect, giving American women nationwide the right to vote.

Norway becomes the first European nation to establish compulsory military service for men and women.

More than 300 women in Hollywood establish Time's Up, with a focus on improving safety and equity in the workplace. The organization collects more than $20 million for a legal defense fund.

ACTIVITIES

Transparency

Timeline

Analyze important historic events relating to gender equality in different cultural, historical, and contemporary contexts.

1. Why might these events be featured in the timeline? What makes these events important?
2. How might people from different social or ideological groups have interpreted these events when they took place?
3. What effect did these events have on people from different social and political groups?
4. How might these events have shaped the world today? What sources can be used to illustrate these effects?
5. How might recent perspectives affect the way people interpret these events?

Quiz

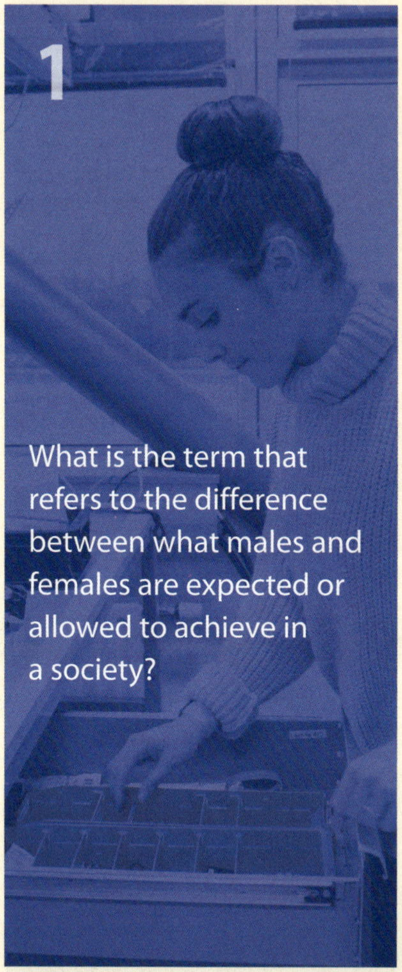

1

What is the term that refers to the difference between what males and females are expected or allowed to achieve in a society?

2

Who was the first female justice on the U.S. Supreme Court?

3 In what year did women achieve full voting rights in Great Britain?

4

What section of the Education Amendments of 1972 requires almost all U.S. schools to offer male and female students equal opportunities to play sports?

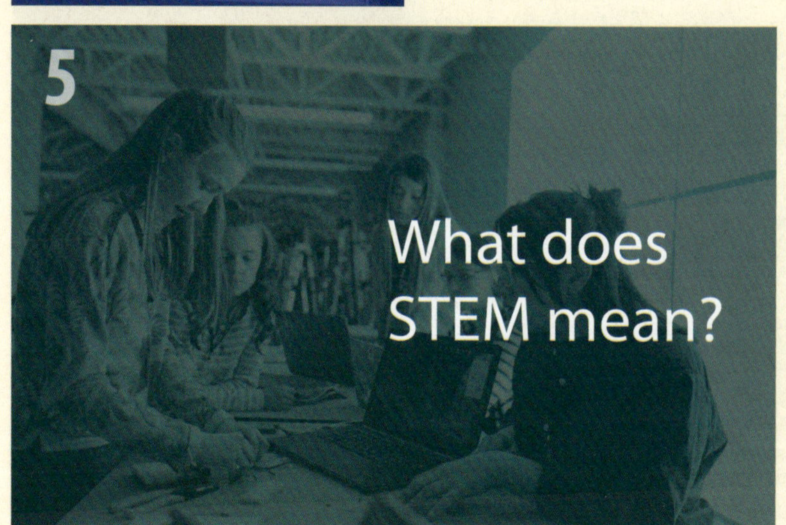

5

What does STEM mean?

6 **What American activist organization was founded in 1966?**

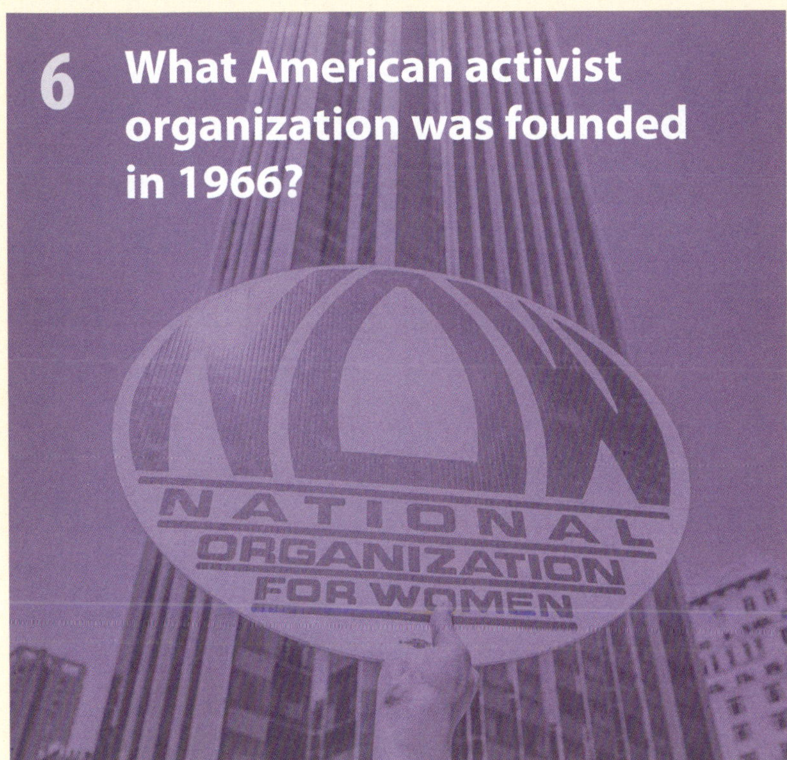

7

How many countries had female heads of state or heads of government in 2017?

8 In what portion of U.S. households are women the primary financial provider?

9

Who was the first woman publisher of a major American newspaper?

10

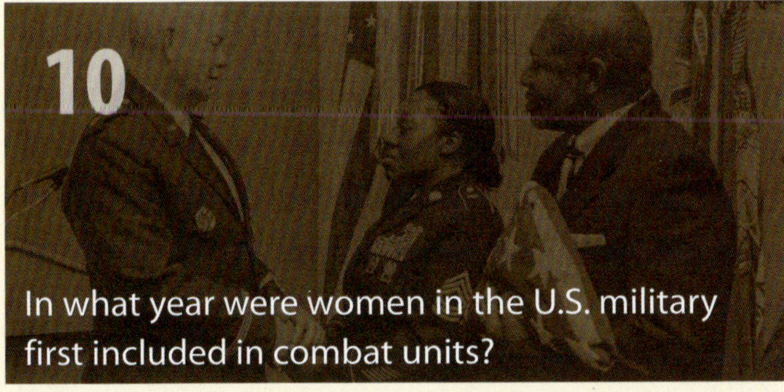

In what year were women in the U.S. military first included in combat units?

ANSWERS

1 gender gap **2** Sandra Day O'Connor
3 1928 **4** Title IX **5** science, technology, engineering, and math
6 National Organization for Women
7 15 **8** about 40 percent
9 Katharine Graham **10** 2015

Key Words

absolute monarchy: a form of government in which a single person, usually a king or queen, rules without constitutional limits

developed countries: countries with high average income and advanced technology

developing countries: countries with low average income that until recently had little manufacturing and technology

expatriate: a person who lives outside his or her country of birth

Fortune 500: a list, compiled annually by *Fortune* magazine, of the 500 largest U.S. corporations in terms of revenue

gender discrimination: treating people unequally because of personal characteristics such as gender that are not related to their performance

gender gap: the difference between what males and females are expected or allowed to achieve in a society

gender-neutral: not related to either males or females

gender rights: equal rights for all members of a society regardless of their gender

gender roles: sets of expected behaviors that a society considers appropriate for male or female

Global South: the developing countries of Africa, Asia, and Latin America

human trafficking: the illegal transporting of people for the purpose of forced labor or other types of exploitation

industrialization: the transformation of social life resulting from the technological and economic developments involving factories

matriarchies: states, societies, communities, or families in which women hold positions of power

norms: set standards in a particular community

objectification: the action of degrading someone to the status of just an object

postcolonial: referring to the period of an area's history after that area stopped being ruled as a colony by another country

suffrage: the right by law to vote in national and local elections

theology: the religious beliefs of a faith or group

unisex: not identifiable as intended either for males or females

Index

LIGHTBOX

SUPPLEMENTARY RESOURCES

Click on the plus icon ⊕ found in the bottom left corner of each spread to open additional teacher resources.

- Download and print the book's quizzes and activities
- Access curriculum correlations
- Explore additional web applications that enhance the Lightbox experience

LIGHTBOX DIGITAL TITLES
Packed full of integrated media

VIDEOS

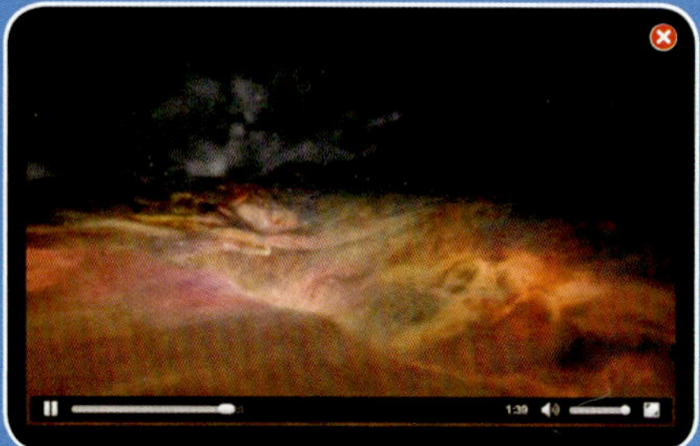

INTERACTIVE MAPS

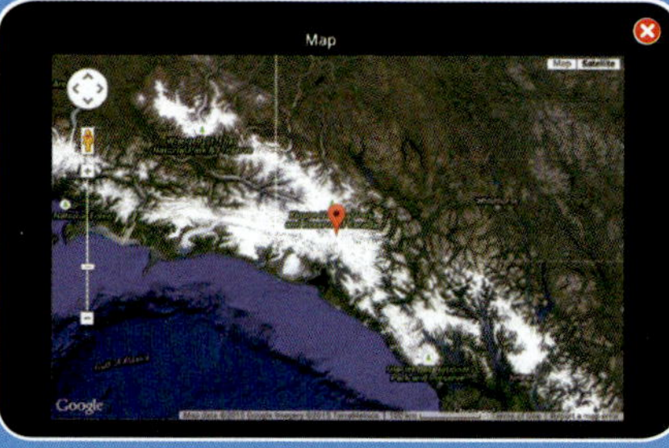

WEBLINKS

SLIDESHOWS

QUIZZES

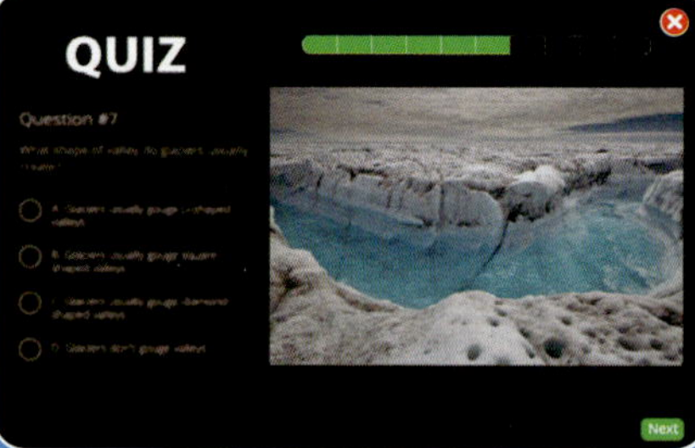

OPTIMIZED FOR

- ✔ TABLETS
- ✔ WHITEBOARDS
- ✔ COMPUTERS
- ✔ AND MUCH MORE!

Published by Smartbook Media Inc.
350 5th Avenue, 59th Floor New York, NY 10118
Website: www.openlightbox.com

First published by Mason Crest in 2017

Library of Congress Control Number: 2018941074

ISBN 978-1-5105-3873-3 (hardcover)
ISBN 978-1-5105-3874-0 (multi-user ISBN)

Printed in Brainerd, Minnesota, United States
1 2 3 4 5 6 7 8 9 0 22 21 20 19 18

062018
150618

Project Coordinator: Heather Kissock
Art Director: Terry Paulhus

Every reasonable effort has been made to trace ownership and to obtain permission to reprint copyright material. The publisher would be pleased to have any errors or omissions brought to its attention so that they may be corrected in subsequent printings.

The publisher acknowledges Getty Images and Alamy as its primary image suppliers for this title.